W9-BTB-360

YES VIRGINIA

THERE IS A SANTA CLAUS

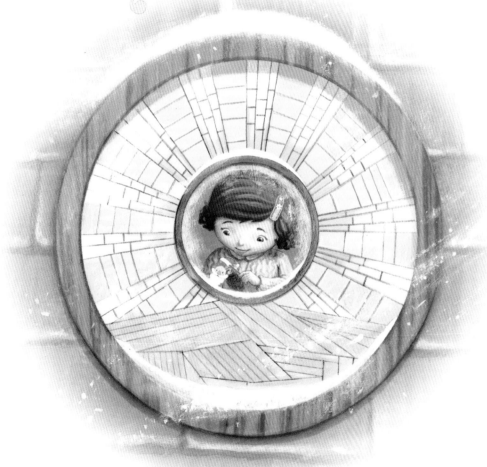

by CHRIS PLEHAL
pictures by JAMES BERNARDIN

HARPER

An Imprint of HarperCollinsPublishers

CHRISTMASTIME is full of joy and happiness . . . usually.

But one year, long ago, Christmas wasn't very happy at all.

Times were hard in New York City, and the weather was especially cold. People hurried through the streets, bundled up against the chill. No one stopped to smile or say hello. Christmas was just a few weeks away, but nobody even seemed to notice.

Nobody, that is, except for a little girl named Virginia.

Virginia loved Christmas. She loved the glittering lights. She loved the joyful carols. But most of all, she loved Santa Claus.

She could hardly wait for Christmas Eve, when she would set out a plate of cookies and listen for sleigh bells. This year, she even made her very own Santa Claus book.

"Wow!" Virginia's best friend Ollie exclaimed as he looked at the book. "We should show Tom! And Taylor! And George! Come on, let's go!"

Virginia was a bit nervous about showing it to *everybody*. But Ollie was already running down the stairs, so Virginia grabbed the book and followed him out the door.

At the park, the other children gathered around to see Virginia's book. Everyone was so excited, they shouted all at once.

"Last year, Santa brought me a train set!" said Tom.

"He brought me a dollhouse!" exclaimed Taylor.

"I got a baseball mitt!" shouted George.

"Did Santa bring you a baby bottle, too?" said a voice.

Charlotte, the meanest, bossiest, snootiest girl in town, pushed her way forward.

"You still believe in Santa?" Charlotte scoffed. "Ha! That's hysterical! No one could travel the whole world in one night!"

"That's not true!" said Virginia. "Santa is as real as you are!"

"It's baby stuff!" teased Charlotte, as she grabbed Virginia's Santa Claus book. With a laugh, she held it high above her head.

"Give it back!" said Virginia.

"Stop it!" shouted Ollie, rushing to help.

But Ollie tripped and bumped into Virginia, who crashed into Charlotte, who lost her grip on Virginia's book . . .

. . . which landed in the mud with a SPLAT.

Charlotte laughed aloud. "Face it, Virginia." She sneered. "There is no Santa Claus!"

Virginia cradled the wet, muddy book in her hands. She knew in her heart that Charlotte was wrong.

"There *is* a Santa Claus," she thought to herself, "and I'm going to prove it!"

That afternoon, Virginia visited a place she knew was full of answers: the New York Public Library.

"Let's see . . . Santa Claus . . . ," said the friendly librarian, as she pulled book after book from the shelves. "Ah! In England his name is Father Christmas!"

"In Holland, he's called Sinterklaas," read Virginia.

"In Italy, he's Babbo Natale!" Ollie cried.

"According to this," said the librarian, flipping through a heavy book, "he lives in Finland. No, wait! Greenland!"

"And he has a giant goat!" Ollie shouted.

Virginia looked at the piles of books on the table. She was frustrated. "This is all interesting," she said, "but none of it tells me if Santa is *real*."

That evening, Virginia passed through Herald Square, in the heart of the city.
A man with a beard and red hat stood on the street corner. Virginia's
heart leaped . . . but the man was skinny and scraggly, and his
beard was tied on with string.

"You're not Santa Claus," Virginia said.

"That's true. I'm not," replied the man.

"Then why are you dressed like him?" Virginia asked.

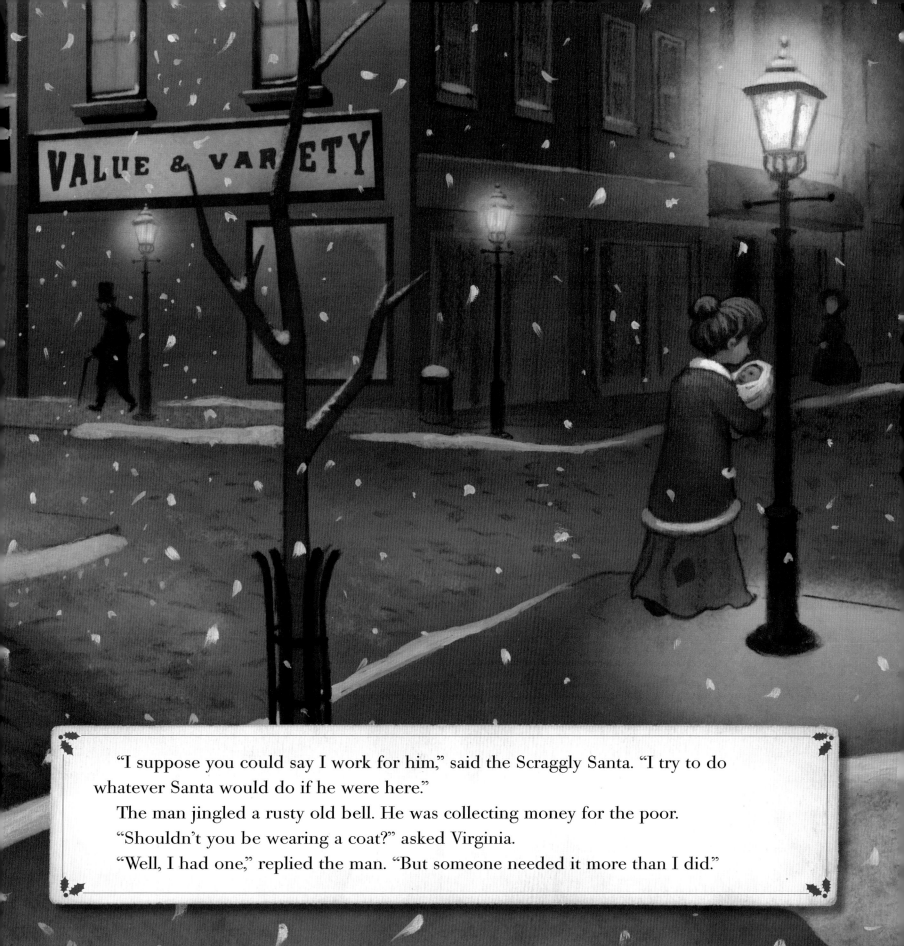

"I suppose you could say I work for him," said the Scraggly Santa. "I try to do whatever Santa would do if he were here."

The man jingled a rusty old bell. He was collecting money for the poor.

"Shouldn't you be wearing a coat?" asked Virginia.

"Well, I had one," replied the man. "But someone needed it more than I did."

That night, Virginia asked her father, "Is there *really* a Santa Claus?"

"Hmm . . . ," he began. "Well, someone brought you presents last year. And someone ate the milk and cookies you left out. So logically . . ."

But Virginia wasn't listening to her father's long-winded explanation. She was looking at something on her father's desk: a copy of the New York *Sun*.

"That's it!" Virginia cried. "I could write to the newspaper!"

"Well, yes, I suppose you could!" said her father. "After all, if you see it in *The Sun*, it's so!"

Virginia went straight to her desk. She took out a pencil and paper. And she began to write a letter.

"Dear Editor," she wrote. "Some of my little friends say there is no Santa Claus. Papa says, 'If you see it in *The Sun*, it's so.' Please tell me the truth: Is there a Santa Claus?"

Virginia smiled. She knew that when *The Sun* received her letter, the editor would surely give her the answer she needed.

A few days later, Virginia's letter arrived at the newspaper office.

"Santa Claus!" growled Francis Church, editor of *The Sun*. "This is preposterous! We report facts, not fantasies!"

"I don't know, sir," said Louis, Mr. Church's assistant. "Maybe you should answer it!"

"Louis, people rely on this paper for the truth," said Mr. Church. "We need to maintain our credibility!"

"But she's only a child," Louis pleaded.

"Everyone grows up sometime," Mr. Church said coldly. He tossed Virginia's letter down the garbage chute, which shut with a loud CLANG.

Meanwhile, Virginia sat in her room and moped. She'd been waiting and waiting, but hadn't heard back from the newspaper.

"I just need some proof!" Virginia sighed.

"Virginia," her mother said, "believing in Santa isn't something you prove. It's something you do. Whenever we act like Santa Claus would, and are kind to others, *that* proves that he's real."

Virginia thought about that. And then she remembered someone *else* who acted like Santa Claus. Suddenly, she had an idea.

The next day, Virginia brought Scraggly Santa a Christmas present.

"A new coat!" he exclaimed. "Just what I needed! Thank you, uh . . . um . . ."

"Virginia," said Virginia.

"Well, Virginia," he replied, "today *you're* Santa Claus."

And even though Scraggly Santa was the one wearing the coat, Virginia felt warm inside.

"Isn't that *adorable*!" said a familiar voice. Virginia turned to see Charlotte standing nearby. On her face was a nasty smile, and in her hand was a crumpled letter.

"I found *this* outside the newspaper office . . . ," Charlotte said, ". . . in a garbage can!"

Virginia felt a hole in the pit of her stomach. The newspaper had thrown her letter away. She couldn't believe it. With tears in her eyes, she ran away as fast as she could.

That night, Scraggly Santa burst into Mr. Church's office.

"This letter was written by a friend of mine," said Scraggly Santa. "I think you'd better answer it."

"I'm sorry, but I only print the facts," replied Mr. Church gruffly.

"When people believe, they make the world a better place," he said. "Answer that letter and you'll give this girl—and maybe this whole city—something to believe in."

That night, Mr. Church didn't go home. Long after everyone else was asleep, he sat in his office, thinking about what Scraggly Santa had said.

"If you see it in *The Sun*," he mumbled to himself, "it's so."

Virginia wasn't sleeping either. She felt like everything she loved—presents, Christmas, Santa Claus—just didn't matter anymore.

"Baby stuff," she sniffed sadly.

The next morning at breakfast, Virginia stared at her porridge. She didn't feel like eating. She didn't feel like doing anything.

Virginia's parents were worried. They had never seen their daughter so upset.

Then there was a knock at the door.

"LOOK!" shouted Ollie as he held up a newspaper.

Virginia gasped as she read the headline. She couldn't believe her eyes. In the paper was an editorial, a message written just for her.

"Virginia, your little friends are wrong. They do not believe except for what they see. Yes, Virginia, there *is* a Santa Claus.

"He exists as certainly as love and generosity and devotion exist. How dreary would be the world if there were no Santa Claus! It would be as dreary as if there were no Virginias.

"There would be no childlike faith then, no poetry, no romance. The eternal light with which childhood fills the world would be extinguished. No Santa Claus? Thank God he lives, and he lives forever! A thousand years from now, Virginia, nay, ten times ten thousand years from now, he will continue to make glad the heart of childhood."

Virginia had never been so happy. There was a magical feeling inside her, bursting to get out.

"Merry Christmas!" she shouted to the street below.

"Merry Christmas," replied an old man who was passing by. He had rosy cheeks, a snowy white beard, and a twinkle in his eye.

The old man reached into his coat and handed something to Virginia. It was her Santa Claus book, good as new.

With a tip of his hat, the old man continued on his way. Virginia smiled as she watched him go. And as she stood on the step, book in hand, Virginia thought the whole world seemed to glow a bit brighter.

The New York Sun

ESTABLISHED 1873   **NEW YORK, NEW YORK**   **PRICE ONE CENT**

Is There a Santa Claus?

Dear Editor:

I am 8 years old. Some of my little friends say there is no Santa Claus. Papa says, "If you see it in THE SUN it's so." Please tell me the truth; is there a Santa Claus?

—Virginia O'Hanlon.

VIRGINIA, your little friends are wrong. They have been affected by the skepticism of a skeptical age. They do not believe except what they see. They think that nothing can be which is not comprehensible by their little minds. All minds, Virginia, whether they be men's or children's, are little. In this great universe of ours man is a mere insect, an ant, in his intellect, as compared with the boundless world about him, as measured by the intelligence capable of grasping the whole of truth and knowledge.

Yes, Virginia, there is a Santa Claus. He exists as certainly as love and generosity and devotion exist, and you know that they abound and give to your life its highest beauty and joy. Alas! how dreary would be the world if there were no Santa Claus. It would be as dreary as if there were no Virginias. There would be no childlike faith then, no poetry, no romance to make tolerable this existence. We should have no enjoyment, except in sense and sight. The eternal light with which childhood fills the world would be extinguished.

Not believe in Santa Claus! You might as well not believe in fairies! You might get your papa to hire men to watch in all the chimneys on Christmas Eve to catch Santa Claus, but even if they did not see Santa Claus coming down, what would that prove? Nobody sees Santa Claus, but that is no sign that there is no Santa Claus. The most real things in the world are those that neither children nor men can see. Did you ever see fairies dancing on the lawn? Of course not, but that's no proof that they are not there. Nobody can conceive or imagine all the wonders there are unseen and unseeable in the world.

You may tear apart the baby's rattle and see what makes the noise inside, but there is a veil covering the unseen world which not the strongest man, nor even the united strength of all the strongest men that ever lived, could tear apart. Only faith, fancy, poetry, love, romance, can push aside that curtain and view and picture the supernal beauty and glory beyond. Is it all real? Ah, Virginia, in all this world there is nothing else real and abiding.

No Santa Claus! Thank God! he lives, and he lives forever. A thousand years from now, Virginia, nay, ten times ten thousand years from now, he will continue to make glad the heart of childhood.

HarperFestival is an imprint of HarperCollins Publishers.

Yes, Virginia

Copyright © 2010 by Macy's. All rights reserved. Printed in the United States of America. No part of this book may be used or reproduced in
any manner whatsoever without written permission except in the case of brief quotations embodied in critical articles and reviews.

For information address HarperCollins Children's Books, a division of HarperCollins Publishers,
10 East 53rd Street, New York, NY 10022.
www.harpercollinschildrens.com

Library of Congress Cataloging-in-Publication Data

Plehal, Christopher J.

Yes, Virginia : based on a true story / Christopher J. Plehal ; illustrated by James Bernardin. — 1st ed.
p. cm.

Summary: In 1897 New York City, a young girl who knows that Santa Claus exists sets out to prove her case to unbelievers by writing a letter
to the editor of the New York *Sun*.

ISBN 978-0-06-200173-3
ISBN 978-0-06-203196-9 (special edition)

1. O'Hanlon, Virginia—Juvenile fiction. [1. O'Hanlon, Virginia—Fiction. 2. Santa Claus—Fiction. 3. Christmas—Fiction. 4. New York (N.Y.)—
History—1865–1898—Fiction.] I. Bernardin, James, ill. II. Title.

PZ7.P7175Yes 2010   2010009387
[E]—dc22   CIP
                                                                                                                    AC

Typography by Tom Starace

10 11 12 13 14 LP/LPR   10 9 8 7 6 5 4 3 2 1
❖
First Edition